MARGRET & H. A. REY'S

Curious George
Votes

Written by Deirdre Langeland

Illustrated in the style of H. A. Rey by Mary O'Keefe Young

HOUGHTON MIFFLIN HARCOURT
Boston   New York

Curious George® is a registered trademark of Houghton Mifflin Harcourt Publishing Company.

hmhbooks.com
curiousgeorge.com

The text of this book is set in Adobe Garamond Pro.
The illustrations are watercolor and charcoal pencil.

ISBN: 978-0-358-24834-7 hardcover
ISBN: 978-0-358-27263-2 paperback

Printed in China
SCP 10 9 8 7 6 5 4 3 2 1
4500799006

George was a good little monkey and always very curious.

One day, George visited the school with his friend, the man with the yellow hat.

"Wait here, George, while I talk to Ms. Wolfe," the man said, "and try to be a good little monkey. I will be back in a few minutes."

George tried his best to sit still. But a school is full of things to interest a curious little monkey.

A class of kids passed by. George wanted to walk in a neat line, too!

The cafeteria buzzed with excitement. Kids were eating their lunches and talking about their favorite animals. They were getting ready to vote for a new school mascot. Each child could choose a single piece of paper with a tiger or owl on it and place it in the ballot box.

At the end of lunch, the animal with the most votes would become the mascot.

The bright posters everywhere were hard for a curious monkey to resist—even one who was trying his best to be good.

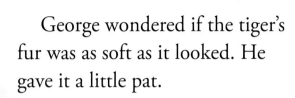

George wondered if the tiger's fur was as soft as it looked. He gave it a little pat.

Oh no! The poster landed in a heap.

He quickly put it back on the wall. But something wasn't right.

George wanted to fix his mistake. On a nearby table, he found a package of markers.

That was better.

On the other side of the cafeteria, George found a girl telling everyone why they should vote for a tiger to be the new school mascot.

"Tigers are strong and fast," she said.

When the girl finished talking, she handed the microphone to a boy. "Those are great points," the boy said, "but I think that an owl would make the best mascot because they can fly."

George wondered how anyone could make a decision when they were both good mascot choices.

George got up and looked
more closely at the posters. He
tried to imagine what it was like
to be an owl flying and hooting.

Then he imagined he was a tiger roaming. He got a little carried away.

Some kids were handing out stickers with their favorite mascots on them. George wanted to be fair, so he took one from each kid.

By the time George had gone all the way around the cafeteria, he was covered from head to toe in tigers and owls.

George was proud of his new stickers. But when he got all the way around the room, he noticed something: the cafeteria was really crowded with everyone getting ready to vote.

The kids couldn't move around as easily as George.

George wanted to make sure every kid got a sticker, so he went through the cafeteria, handing them out.

George made his way back to the front of the cafeteria. On the table with the markers, there was a big, strange box. It had a slot in the top. George watched carefully as a girl picked up a piece of paper and dropped the paper into the ballot box. George liked the way the paper rustled as it slid in. That looked like fun!

George wanted to try it, but instead of picking his choice for mascot, George drew his own picture of the animal, like he had before on the back of the tiger poster.

Then he dropped in one ballot. It hit the bottom of the box with a little *plunk*.

He dropped three more in—all at once.
Schwick! They just fit through the slot.

He wondered how many ballots
he could fit into the box.

As it turned out, he could fit a lot.

Mr. Windle came to pick up the ballot box. It was time to count the votes and find out what the new school mascot would be. But something was very strange about the ballots. He separated the votes into piles.

One pile for each animal, and one for George's doodled ballots.

Mr. Windle was not amused. "Why are there so many papers in the ballot box? And why are there so many with extra doodles and drawings?"

George was worried. He hadn't meant to cause trouble. But then a girl spoke up. "It was George," she said. "But he was only being curious. And he was very helpful, too! He acted out the animals for us and gave everyone campaign stickers.

"He also made us laugh a lot. We learned about write-in votes and how, if we want, we can write in our choice for the vote instead of picking one of the two choices."

"Well, that explains the ballots with the different doodles on them," Mr. Windle said. "But it also explains the most votes."

"There are fifteen votes for the owls, ten for the tigers . . . and twenty write-in votes for the monkeys! A monkey will be a good mascot because they are curious about the world."

George and the kids ate pudding cups to celebrate the new mascot.

In honor of the new mascot, the teachers decided to have bookmarks made with a monkey on them. They could sell the bookmarks to help raise money to buy a costume for the new mascot.

And that's how George got to cheer for himself
at the first baseball game of the season.